Ripper and Fang

One dog smiled at Dan. It was medium-sized, with brown curly fur and a tail that went round and round as if it was about to go into orbit.

"I'll take that one, please," said Dan.

More Young Hippo Animal stories for animal-lovers!

Hands Off Our Hens!
Jennifer Curry

Big Puss, Little Mouse
Kara May

Join The Petsitters Club for ANIMAL ADVENTURE!

Tessa Krailing

Margaret D. Clark

Ripper and Fang

Illustrated by Ann James

Hippo

Scholastic Children's Books
Commonwealth House, 1-19 New Oxford Street
London WC1A 1NU, UK
a division of Scholastic Ltd
London ~ New York ~ Toronto ~ Sydney ~ Auckland

First published in Australia by Omnibus Books,
part of the Ashton Scholastic Group, 1992
Published in the UK by Scholastic Ltd, 1997

ISBN 0 590 13636 4

Typeset by Backup Creative Services, Dorset
Printed by Cox & Wyman Ltd, Reading, Berks.

2 4 6 8 10 9 7 5 3 1

Chapter 1

Plan A

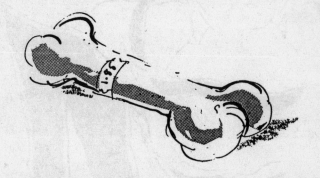

"It's not fair!"

Dan stamped his foot and pulled a
terrible face. His mum and dad took
no notice. They had made up their
minds. No dog!

But Dan was determined to get a dog of his own. He had already picked out a name, Ripper, because it would be a *ripper* of a dog: medium-sized, with brown curly fur and a tail that went round and round like a helicopter rotor. It was his dream.

But dreams don't come true unless you have plans.

PLAN A

- Buy a dog collar,
- a lead
- two bowls (food and water)
- a blanket
- a kennel
- flea powder
- dog soap
- dog toys
- dog food

Dan took ten pounds from his
special money container and hurried
down the street to the pet shop.

The pet shop had everything you could need for a dog, but it was all so expensive. Dan could only afford a collar, some flea powder, a cake of dog soap and a rubber bone.

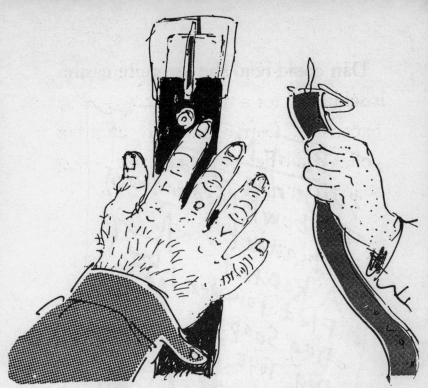

As Dan reached out to select a plain red collar, another hand – with dirty fingernails and the letters L.O.V.E. tattooed on the fingers – reached out for a big black collar with spiky silver studs. The hand belonged to a tough-looking biker. The other hand held a list.

Dan could read the list quite easily.
It said:

PLAN A
Buy a dog collar
Two bowls (food and water)
A blanket
A Kennel
Flea Powder
Dog Soap
Dog Toys
Dog Food

Wow, thought Dan. He must be getting a dog too.

The biker chose the biggest kennel in the shop. "It won't fit on the bike," he said. "Send it to 451 High Street."

Chapter 2

Plan B

Back home, Dan hid the collar, the flea powder, the soap and the bone in his undies drawer. It was time for Plan B.

Dan found everything he needed in the garage. He borrowed his dad's Instant Everlasting Wonder Glue and stuck three pieces of wood together to make the sides of the kennel. He was very careful not to get glue on his fingers.

The sides were a bit crooked, but he was still able to nail on the sheets of tin for the kennel roof. Then he sprayed the roof with dark green paint and sprayed the sides with yellow paint. Some went on his mum's car, but you couldn't see the specks unless you looked closely.

While the paint was drying, Dan went back to Plan A. He found two bowls in the kitchen. He found an old blanket and a length of rope (for a lead) in the cupboard, and in the pantry he found some tins of Irish stew and curried sausages for tasty dog food.

Chapter 3

Plan C

Now he was ready for Plan C.

PLAN C
1. Catch the bus to the Dog's' Home
2. Choose Ripper the dream dog.
3. Bring him home.

He was certain that as soon as his mum and dad saw Ripper, and saw that everything was ready for him, they would change their minds and let him stay.

Dan ran round the corner to the High Street and caught the Number 7 bus. He hurried because he didn't want his mum and dad to see what he was doing. (He wasn't supposed to travel alone on buses!)

As the bus drove off, he saw the biker from the pet shop leaping up and down on the kick-start of his big shiny motor bike. It was a great bike. It even had a sidecar for passengers.

The bus and the motor bike arrived at the Dogs' Home together, and Dan and the biker walked in side by side.

"Can I help you?" asked the manager of the Dogs' Home.

"I want a ripper of a dog, medium-sized, with brown curly fur and a tail that goes round and round like a helicopter rotor," said Dan.

"I want the biggest, meanest, blackest dog in the place to guard my bike," said the biker.

There were all sorts of dogs.
Some looked eager.

Can YOU read four Young Hippo books?

The Young Hippo is sending a special prize to everyone who collects any four of these stickers, which can be found in Young Hippo books.

This is one sticker to stick on your own Young Hippo Readometer Card!

Collect four stickers and fill up your Readometer Card

There are all these stickers to collect too!

Get your Young Hippo Readometer Card from your local bookshop, or by sending your name and address to:

Some looked sad.

Some looked haughty.

Some looked *bad*.

Chapter 4

Dream Dogs

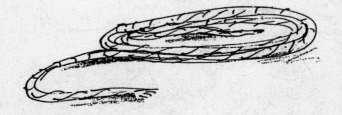

One dog smiled at Dan. It was medium-sized, with brown curly fur and a tail that went round and round as if it was about to go into orbit.

"I'll take that one, please," said Dan.

"And I'll take *that* one," said the biker, pointing to a big, mean-looking black dog with five notches in its tail and a torn ear. "It looks like a *killer*."

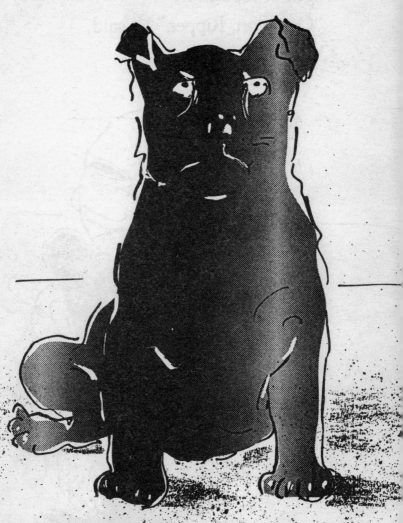

Both Dan and the biker paid for their dogs. Dan put the new red collar around Ripper's neck and tied the length of rope to it.

"Come on, Ripper," he said.

The biker put the big black collar with the spiky silver studs around his dog's neck and clipped on a heavy chain.

"Come on, Fang," he said.

Dan and Ripper went to climb aboard the Number 7 bus.

"No dogs allowed," said the driver.

It was a long walk home.

"Where are you going?" asked the biker, riding up to him on his motor bike, with Fang in the sidecar. When Dan told him, he said, "That's just round the corner from my house, in the next street. I've moved into the blue bungalow with the green roof."

"Oh," said Dan. "That's the house behind ours."

"Hop in the sidecar," said the biker.

"I can't," said Dan. "I'm not allowed to go anywhere with strangers."

"What's the matter?" asked a policeman, pulling up on his motor bike.

Dan explained the problem.

"It's all right," said the policeman. "This is Basil, and he works part-time in my cousin's garage. He's okay. But I'll follow you, so you know you'll be safe."

So Dan lifted Ripper into the sidecar with Fang, and then climbed in too. They roared down the road, going flat out.

Dan arrived home safely and took Ripper straight inside. What would his parents say?

Chapter 5

He's a Ripper All Right!

He kept Ripper on the rope while his
mum and dad stared, amazed. At first
they were cross, but they soon gave in,
especially when they saw the kennel,
the bowls, the blanket, the flea
powder, the soap and the bone.

"He can stay," said Dad. "You've earned the right to have a dog."

"That's great!" said Dan. "Thanks!"
And he let Ripper off the rope.

"He's a ripper all right," said Mum, as Ripper started ripping the sofa to shreds.

"He's a ripper for sure," said Dad, as Ripper sank sharp teeth into his trouser leg, ripping the material.

"Perhaps I should call him something else," said Dan, as Ripper tried to rip off his fingers.

"Don't bother thinking up a new name," said Dad, as Ripper ripped through the back door. "I've changed my mind. *He's not staying.*"

Dan followed Ripper outside, in time to see him ripping chunks off the new dog kennel. Dan was upset. Ripper had fooled him well and truly.

Then Ripper started barking, a blood-curdling sound that made Dan's hair stand on end. It was going to be a noisy night.

Chapter 6

You Wimp!

Next morning, Ripper had gone. He'd
tunnelled right under the back fence.

Oh, *no*, thought Dan. What's he
ripping up now?

Just as he was about to climb up the fence for a look, a big black dog jumped over his head, landing on Dad's cabbages and squashing them flat.

"Go on then, you wimp," yelled a voice, and Basil the biker poked his head over the fence.

"Huh," he said. "I wish I'd chosen *your* dog instead of that big coward. Your dog would rip off a robber's arm if he tried to steal my bike."

"Erp," said Dan, because the big black dog was trying to lick his face. The short, stubby tail with the five notches in it was whizzing around like ten helicopter rotors.

Dan looked at Fang. Then he whispered something to Basil, who looked really pleased.

So the big black dog moved in to live with Dan, and became his best friend. And Ripper lived happily ever after with Basil, looking after his bike for him and ripping holes in his jeans and shirts to make them trendy.

The End